DAYDREAMERS

D1538044

IF I WENT SAILING OUT TO SEA

Written and Illustrated by J. Ellen Dolce

MODERN PUBLISHING
A Division of Unisystems, Inc.
New York, New York 10022

If I went sailing
out to sea . . .

an octopus would
play with me.

And if I went camping
by a lake . . .

I'd make popcorn, fries
and cake.

Well, if I went diving
way down deep . . . .

I'd discover where
the mermaids sleep.

But, if I went on a trip
to the moon . . .

I'd float up high in
a big balloon.

If I went exploring
in a cave . . .

I'd bring my bear,
who's very brave.

And if I went searching for buried gold . . .

I'd dig until the day
grew old.

Well, if I went skating on the ice . . .

I'd glide along
     with a troop of mice.

But, we go skipping
off to school . . .

where we always follow
every rule.